For Anna, with love x
- T C

For Tim
- J C

LITTLE TIGER PRESS LTD,
an imprint of the Little Tiger Group
1 Coda Studios, 189 Munster Road, London SW6 6AW
www.littletiger.co.uk

First published in Great Britain 2016
This edition published 2018

Text copyright © Tracey Corderoy 2016
Illustrations copyright © Jane Chapman 2016
Visit Jane Chapman at www.ChapmanandWarnes.com
Tracey Corderoy and Jane Chapman have asserted their rights to be identified as the author
and illustrator of this work under the Copyright, Designs and Patents Act, 1988
A CIP catalogue record for this book is available from the British Library
All rights reserved

ISBN 978-1-78881-041-8
LTP/2700/2736/0319
Printed in China
4 6 8 10 9 7 5 3

Squish Squash Squeeze!

Tracey Corderoy   Jane Chapman

LiTTLE TiGER

LONDON

Mouse's new house had
shady trees and a roof like a witch's hat.
It had creaky steps, and flowerpots,
and pegs for muddy boots.

"Oooh!"

cried Mouse as he marched on in.

"It's just right!"

Mouse quickly shooed the cobwebs away.
"And LOOK – a piano!"
he smiled.

He jumped
right up and
started to play –

Plink-plonk! Plink-plonk! Plink-plonk!

But all of a sudden . . .

"ROARRRRR!"

A big brown bear burst out!

"I'm a scary bear in a scary house and there's
NO ROOM HERE, not even for a mouse!"

Mouse folded his arms.

"You don't scare ME, Mr Grumble-Pants!

There's **plenty** of room – so no more stuff and nonsense!"

With that, Mouse started to unpack his books.

"Bear - you can help too!" he said.

Mouse skipped up his 'just right' stairs –
all the way to the bathroom!
But when he peeped
round the door . . .

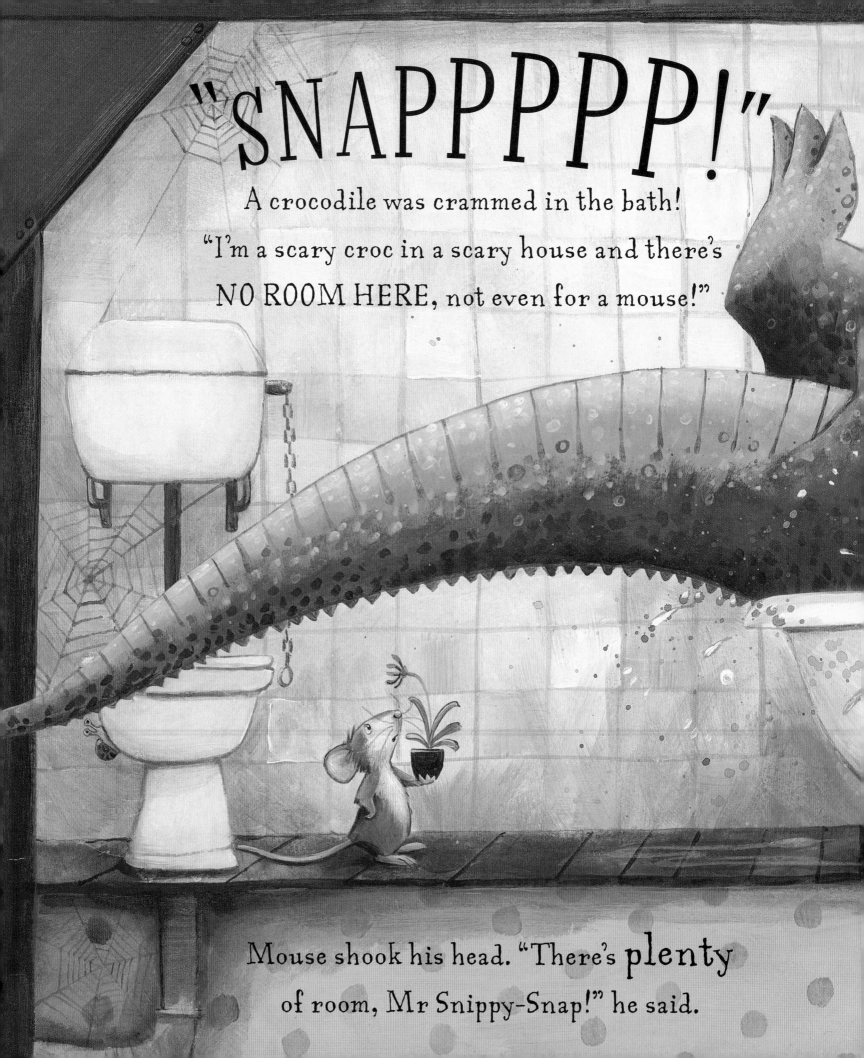

"SNAPPPPP!"

A crocodile was crammed in the bath!

"I'm a scary croc in a scary house and there's **NO ROOM HERE**, not even for a mouse!"

Mouse shook his head. "There's **plenty** of room, Mr Snippy-Snap!" he said.

"Now, my plant needs a drink – so please turn on that tap.
And no more stuff and nonsense!"

Bit by bit,

Mouse squeezed all his things

into the tiny house.

"Only **two** more boxes!"

he said, trotting through the hall.

But before he could unpack them, he heard a huge . . .

WHOOSH!

...and a tiger came whizzing down the banister!

"I'm a scary – EEEK!" the tiger squealed as he
flew off the end and . . .

CRASH!

"NOW look what you've done!" grumbled Bear.

"There's no ROOM to be untidy!" snapped Crocodile.

"I just went too fast," Tiger sighed. "Sorry."

It was quite a mess.

"Right!" said Mouse. "No more stuff and nonsense!

Let's all tidy up – then we can have some tea."

With a wiggle and a jiggle and a squish–squash–squeeze,
there was just enough room for the four of them.

"Budge up a bit, Bear!" Tiger tutted.

"Move your tail, Tiger!" grumbled Bear.

"I need the LOO!" squeaked Crocodile. "Let me through!"

Just then, there was a strange RUMMMBLE
underneath the floor.

"Oh, my!" cried Mouse. "What was that?!"

"It sounded like something BIG!" gulped Bear.

"And SCARY!" gasped Tiger.

RUMBLE-THRUMBLE-THUMP!

"It's coming nearer!" Crocodile cried, his teeth chattering.
The noise grew RUMBLIER and THRUMBLIER until
the teacups jumped in their saucers!

"It sounds like it's in our house," Tiger trembled.

"What if IT wants to live here too?!"

There was only one thing for it.

Mouse stood tall and called in his biggest,

bravest voice . . .

"I'm a **scary** mouse, in a **scary**

house and there's no—"

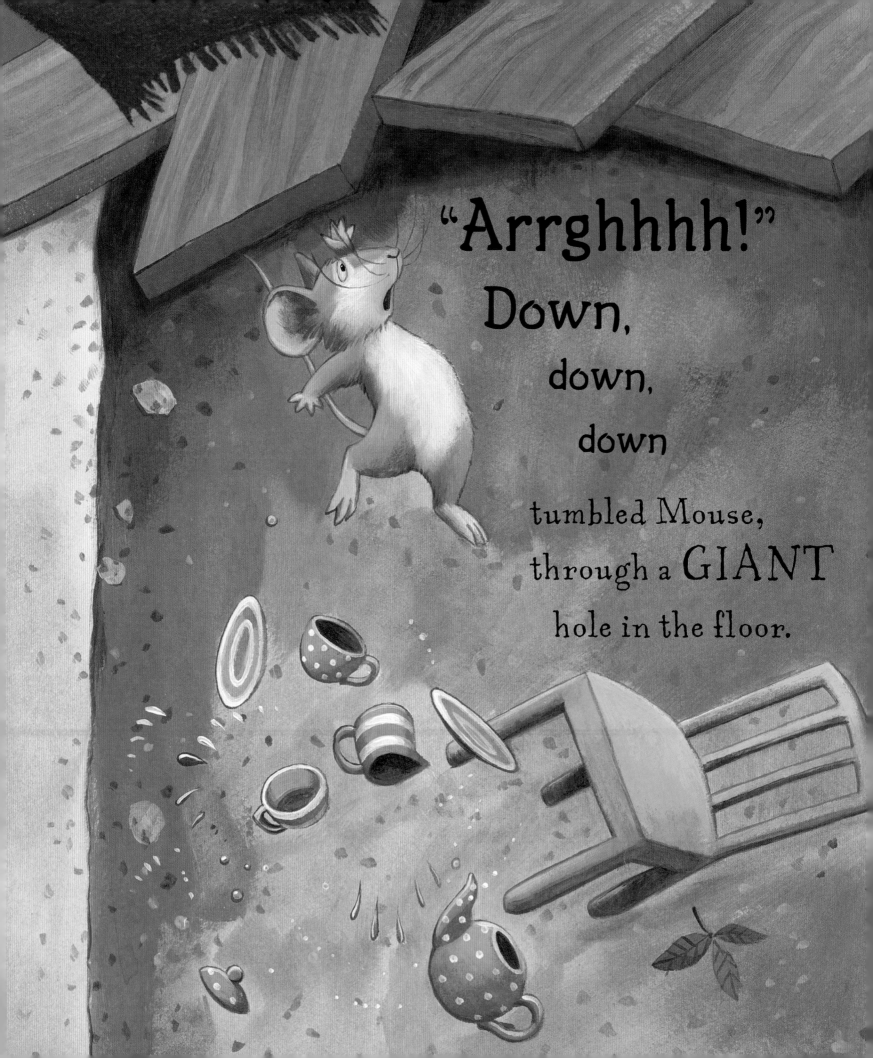

"Arrghhhh!" Down, down, down tumbled Mouse, through a GIANT hole in the floor.

He landed - BUMP! - and looked around.

"Ooopsy!" said a little mole, blinking at the RUMPUS he'd caused.

"I must have dug a bit too much. And now I've made this great big hole under your house! I'm so sorry!"

But Mouse started to smile.

"Stuff and nonsense!" he said. "It's just what we need!"

And with a wiggle and a jiggle,

this time there REALLY was . . .

. . . plenty of room for

EVERYONE!